P9-DGZ-418

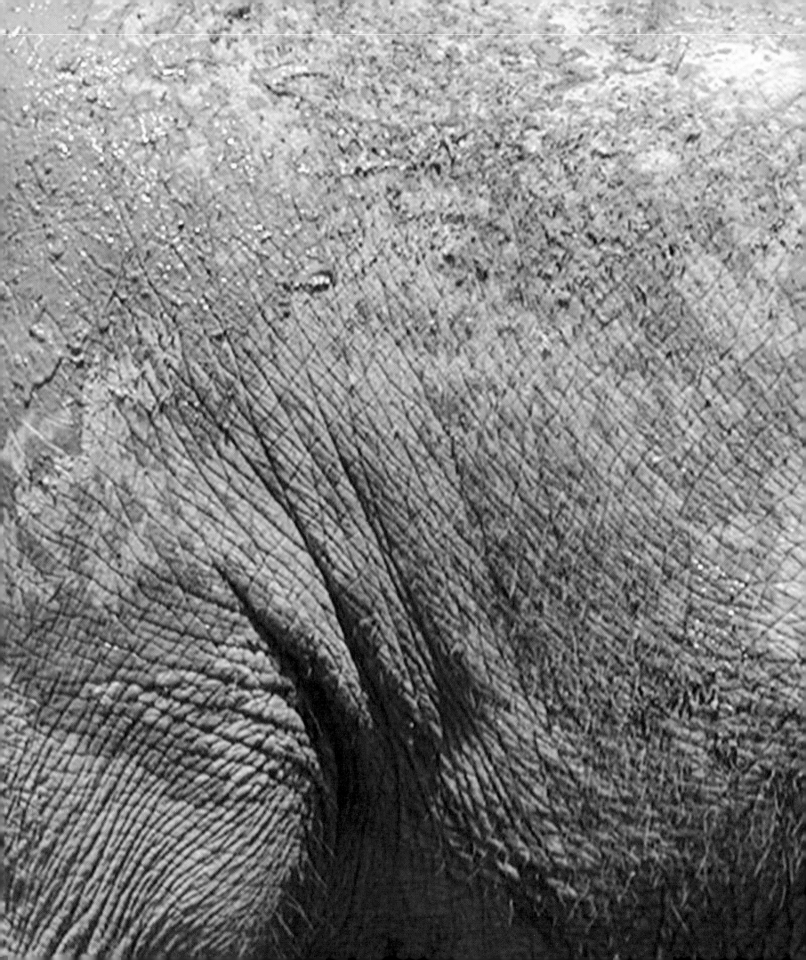

JUST FOR ELEPHANTS Carol Buckley

TILBURY HOUSE PUBLISHERS, GARDINER, MAINE

The day had finally arrived. Shirley was about to leave the zoo where she had lived

for many years. Everyone was happy for her because she was going to the Elephant

Sanctuary, a special place just for elephants. But some of the zookeepers had tears

in their eyes. They would miss their old elephant friend.

A big truck with a special trailer pulled up outside Shirley's barn at the zoo.

The driver was ready to go. "Let's load her up," he said.

It had been a long time since Shirley had ridden in a trailer. The last time was twenty-three years ago, when she had to leave the circus and her elephant friends. Shirley's leg had been broken in a bad accident with another elephant, and the circus decided to sell her to a zoo because she could no longer perform tricks.

It took a lot of patience and treats to get Shirley up into the special trailer. Solomon, who had been her zookeeper for almost all of her years at the zoo, climbed into the cab of the truck with the driver. Shirley looked out the window as they started down the road. She didn't know that in a few hours she would start a new life where she could finally be with other elephants and roam freely, just as she pleased.

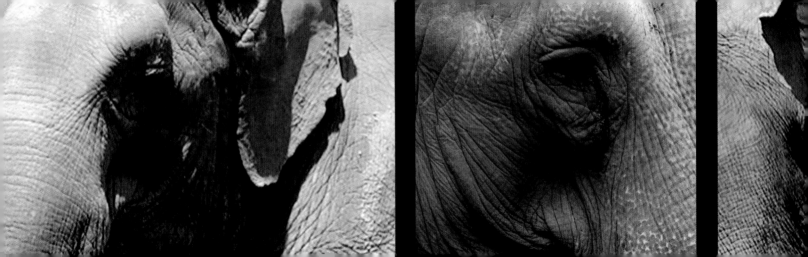

When the trailer stopped
moving hours later, it was
dark, Shirley could smell
something familiar and hear
sounds that she recognized.
There were other elephants
nearby—and they were
talking to her! She looked
out through the trailer
door, and in the darkness

Solomon helped lead Shirley out of the trailer and into her new barn. Elephants sometimes need a little time to get used to new elephants, so Shirley was in a fenced-off part of the barn at first. When Solomon helped take the chain off Shirley's leg, he gave her a big hug. With tears in his eyes he said, "Shirley, you're going to be free, now."

As Shirley began to explore her new barn, some of the elephants greeted her through the bars. Then an elephant named Jenny came into the barn and walked right up to Shirley, as if she had known her for years. She tried to reach through the fence to touch Shirley, and then she tried to climb over the bars!

Suddenly Shirley realized that Jenny had been a baby elephant in her circus many years ago. The two elephants trumpeted and cried big elephant tears of joy—they were very happy to be together again after so many years. They struggled to open the gate themselves, and we quickly opened it for them. For the rest of the night they stood close together, touching each other affectionately or resting with their trunks wrapped around each other. These two old friends were too happy to sleep.

The next morning, Jenny led Shirley outside. Shirley had never been free to roam

before. At the Elephant Sanctuary there are hundreds of acres of fields, hills,

forests, and ponds to explore. Jenny and Shirley started their first morning together

with a quick bath in the creek. Then, when Jenny settled in for her usual morning

nap, Shirley took one careful step and stood over her, just the way a mother

elephant does to protect her sleeping baby.

While Jenny slept, one of the other elephants, Tarra, came up to Shirley and touched her softly with her trunk, getting to know her. All of the elephants could see that Shirley and Jenny loved each other, and they slowly began making friends with Shirley, too. In the wild, the female elephants live in herds with their relatives. The elephants at the Sanctuary had formed a family of their own.

Later, all the elephants went to graze out on the open pastures. Shirley was curious and kept moving, eagerly exploring her new home. Jenny stayed close by her side, and Tarra was never far behind. We were keeping an eye on Shirley, to see how she liked her new home. It was exciting for us to see her so free.

In the afternoon, the elephants grazed their way towards the upper pond. Elephants love to swim, and Jenny had led Shirley to her favorite swimming hole. At the water's edge the elephants splashed water on their backs to cool down. Jenny and Shirley stepped into the pond, ankle deep, and then ventured deeper. They dunked their faces under the water and sprayed each other. They began to play elephant games, rolling around and pushing each other all the way under the water. They had a wonderful time!

After their swim, the elephants used their trunks to cover their wet bodies with dirt to protect their skin from bug bites and sunburn. Then they found a comfortable place to lie down for a group nap. Pretty soon all that could be heard were some redtail hawks screeching overhead and the snoring of many contented elephants.

As the sun began to set, Jenny started back towards the barn, showing the way, and Shirley followed. They stopped here and there to graze on pasture grasses. They ate some persimmons that had fallen from the trees and grazed on river cane and china grass that grow wild. When they met up with other elephants, they shared excited trumpet calls and gentle touching with their trunks. Everyone welcomed the newcomer into the family.

Once the elephants returned to the barn, Scott and I put out the evening meal—

fresh hay, grain, fruits, and vegetables—and filled the water troughs. We stood

together and watched Shirley, to see how she felt about her first day of freedom.

She slowly walked over to the food that was laid out for her and began to eat.

Then she stopped for a moment. She raised her eyes to gaze at us and gave

a mighty elephant trumpet. The other elephants gathered around her touching,

chirping, and trumpeting their own excitement. Shirley had a new home and

a new family, in a place just for elephants.

HOW THE SANCTUARY GOT STARTED:

In 1995, after Carol Buckley had spent more than twenty years working in circuses and zoos with her elephant Tarra, she decided elephants deserved a different life. With Scott Blais, who had also been working with elephants, she decided to create the Elephant Sanctuary on 100 acres of land they purchased in Hohenwald, Tennessee. They dreamed of a place where elephants could just be elephants, where abused elephants could find a haven, and where old elephants could live out their days peacefully. Over the years, the Sanctuary has grown to become a 2,700-acre natural-habitat refuge. There is now enough room at the Sanctuary for as many as 100 elephants. Nineteen elephants are in residence now. The Sanctuary is located in the heart of Tennessee, 85 miles southwest of Nashville. It is just for elephants and is not open to the public. To learn more about the life Tarra and Carol led before the Sanctuary, read *Travels with Tarra* published by Tilbury House in 2002.

KEEPING ELEPHANTS HAPPY AND HEALTHY:

Like most animals, elephants need food, companionship, freedom of movement, and a sense of security to be happy. But their majestic size (they are the largest land mammal) creates other requirements. In the wild, elephants sleep very little and are in motion for eighteen hours each day. This constant movement over soft ground (versus concrete) keeps their feet, joints, and digestive systems healthy. Elephants in the wild can live seventy years or more. At the Elephant Sanctuary, elephants have many acres to roam. Plenty of "space" also helps elephants adjust as new members join their herd, and the relaxed environment has changed "difficult" elephants into calm, contented members of the herd. Since it is the goal of the Elephant Sanctuary to provide a life for its elephants that is as close to "wild" as possible, the approach the caregivers use to work with the elephants is to "go to the elephant," rather than have the elephant always come into the barn for any necessary medical treatment or extra food. Carol Buckley, Scott Blais, and others whose life work is connected to the well-being of animals say it's time to change the way we humans relate to animals. They feel that people should think of themselves as "animal caregivers" rather than as "animal owners." Then other attitudes will change, and the result will be that animals everywhere will lead better lives.

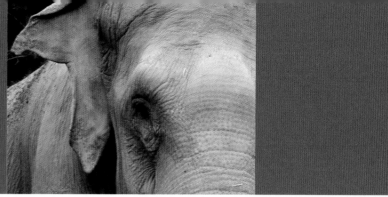

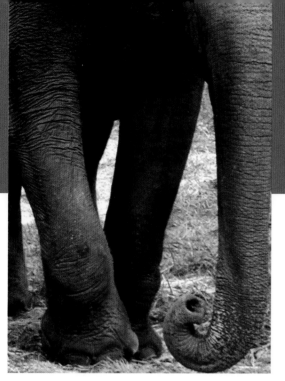

WHY THE ELEPHANT SANCTUARY HAS A "LADIES ONLY" RULE:

Elephants are matriarchal by nature; they live in herds of related females. The only males in the herd are young males who still need their mothers. Usually the males are ready to leave the herd between six and ten years of age. Young males will change groups many times before they reach adulthood, at which time males lead a semi-solitary life. Adult female and male elephants do not live together in the wild.

AN ELEPHANT NEVER FORGETS—REALLY!

Elephants form intricate family structures. They grieve for their dead in a more-than-instinctive way. They show humor and express compassion for one another with intense interactions. They often have a "best friend." The story of Shirley and Jenny's reunion is just one example. You can learn more about elephant interaction by visiting the Elephant Sanctuary's website at www.elephants.com, where you can also watch streaming video footage through the "elecam."

MORE ABOUT SHIRLEY:

When Shirley was working in a circus many years ago, she was aboard a circus ship that caught fire in Nova Scotia. Even though the ship sank, almost all of the animals were rescued. But Shirley has scars from burns during the accident. Her ear was damaged many years before in a fight with another circus elephant. Shirley is one of the oldest elephants in her adopted family at the Sanctuary, and she is the reigning matriarch. Shirley was caught in the wild in Sumatra over fifty years ago. She is also one of the Sanctuary's largest elephants. Shirley is nearly nine feet tall and she weighs 9,200 pounds. Apples are her favorite food.

MORE ABOUT JENNY:

Jenny was caught in the wild in Sumatra over thirty years ago and spent her entire captive life performing in circuses. In April 1995 Jenny was left at a dilapidated animal shelter near Las Vegas. She was severely underweight, and had developed chronic foot rot. Afraid and shy when she first arrived at the Sanctuary, she visibly relaxed when Tarra (the Sanctuary's first resident) gently stroked her head with her trunk and finally coaxed her to entwine trunks! Jenny is just over eight feet tall, she weighs 6,500 pounds, and her favorite food is potatoes.

ADDITIONAL ELEPHANT EDUCATION INFORMATION:

The Elephant Sanctuary website offers downloadable curriculum materials and links on elephants. www.elephants.com. It's a great website!

TILBURY HOUSE, PUBLISHERS

2 Mechanic Street

Gardiner, Maine 04345

800-582-1899

www.tilburyhouse.com

First hardcover printing: November 2006 10 9 8 7 6 5 4 3 2

I would like to thank Shirley and her family for their love and inspiration—without them this book would never have been written. Their deep connection to the earth and keen awareness of themselves and others has had a profound impact on my life and my work. The duality of purpose—mine to serve and theirs to recover and rediscover themselves—makes me realize how connected we all are. My life is blessed by the presence of elephants. —CB

Library of Congress Cataloging-in-Publication Data

Buckley, Carol, 1954-

Just for elephants / Carol Buckley. — 1st hardcover ed.

p. cm.

ISBN-13: 978-0-88448-283-3 (hardcover : alk. paper)

ISBN-10: 0-88448-283-9 (hardcover)

1. Elephants—Tennessee—Hohenwald Region—Juvenile literature. 2. Elephant Sanctuary (Tenn.)—Juvenile literature. I. Title.

QL737.P98B818 2006

639.97'96709768—dc22   2006022283

Designed by Geraldine Millham, Westport, Massachusetts

Color scan restoration work by Pure Photographic Goodness, Portland, Maine

Printed and bound by Sung In Printing, South Korea

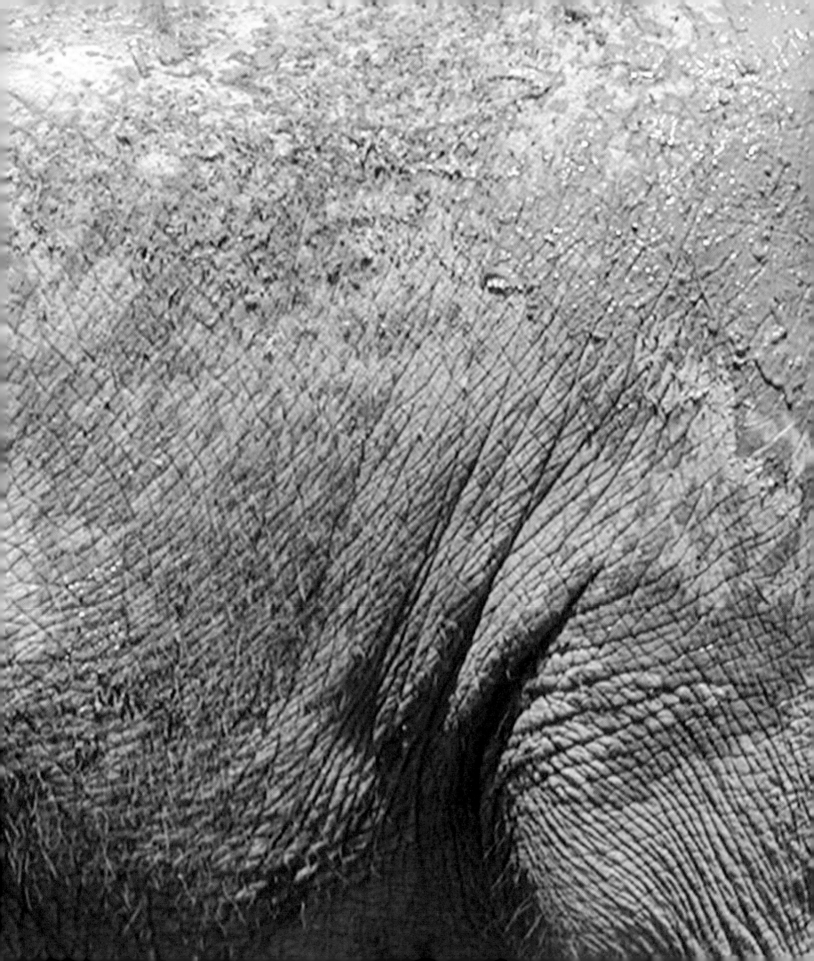

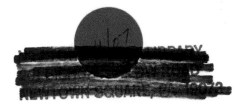